In loving memory of Don Harvey,
and family Chris-Craft rides at Spirit Lake —J. W. H.

For Sam —G.M.

The author donates her proceeds to CALL OF THE SEA,
an educational nonprofit that gives Bay Area youth an
opportunity to sail traditional tall ships, investigate the
local marine environment, connect to the Bay's rich
maritime history, and inspire them to be stewards of the
sea and earth. www.callofthesea.org

Text copyright © 2018 by Jeanne Walker Harvey
Illustrations copyright © 2018 by Grady McFerrin
Book design by Melissa Nelson Greenberg

Library of Congress Control Number
Catologing-in-Publication information available.
ISBN: 978-1-944903-33-6

Printed in China.

10 9 8 7 6 5 4 3 2 1

Cameron Kids is an imprint of
CAMERON + COMPANY

CAMERON + COMPANY
Petaluma, California
www.cameronbooks.com

BOATS ON THE BAY

words by *Jeanne Walker Harvey* • pictures by *Grady McFerrin*

cameron kids

Boats on the bay get ready for the day.

A houseboat rocks by a dock.

A fishing boat slogs through the fog.

A ferry carries passengers.

A sailboat sets sail.

A kayak slides by sea lions.

A tugboat lugs big ships.

A tall ship takes a trip to sea.

A water taxi zigs and zags.

A dredger scoops up mud and muck.

A container ship loads cargo.

A fireboat fans water high and wide.

A sparkling boat joins a parade.

A barge sets off fiery fireworks.

A houseboat rocks by a dock.

Boats on the bay, home for the day.

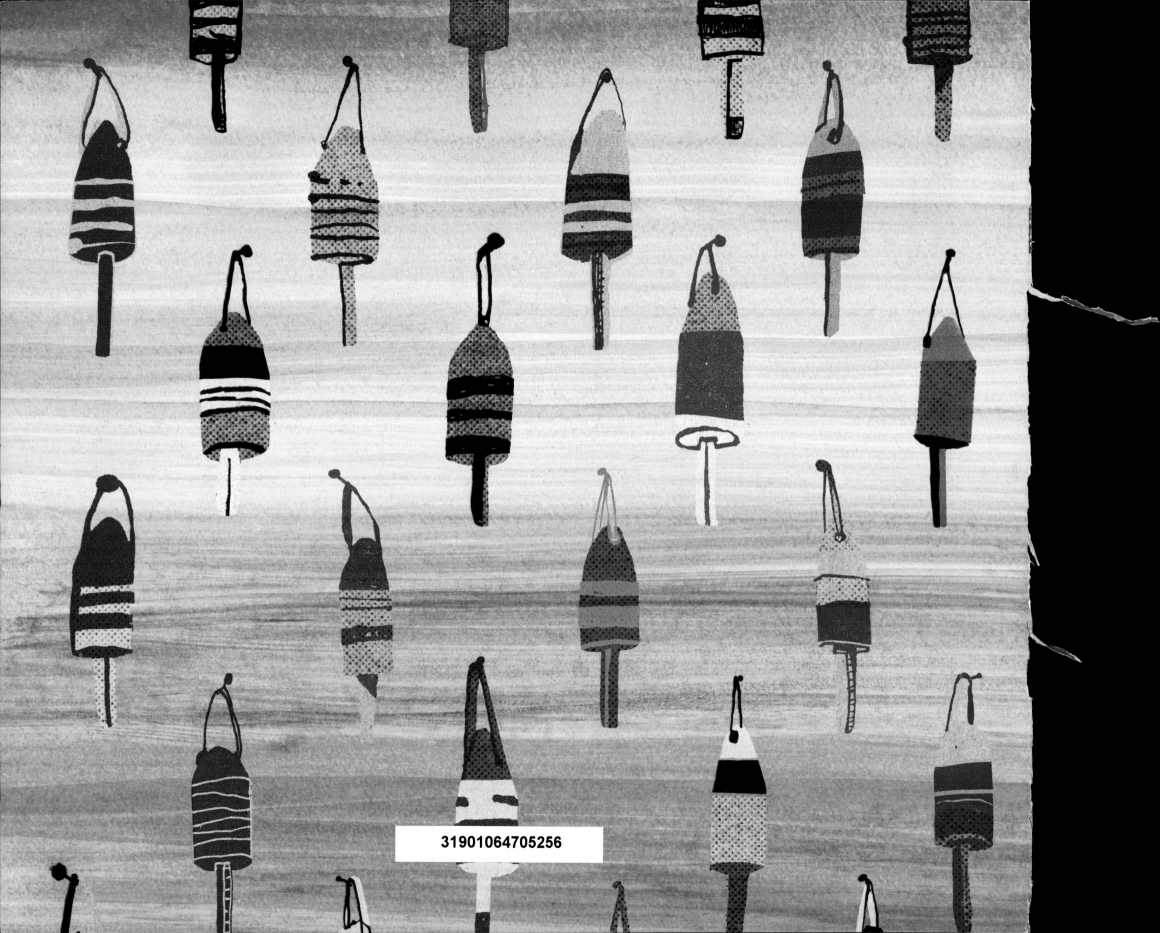